MR PEEK
AND THE MISUNDERSTANDING
AT THE ZOO

FOR MY
PARENTS

A TEMPLAR BOOK

First published in the UK in 2008 by Templar Publishing
This softback edition published in 2009 by Templar Publishing,
an imprint of The Templar company Limited,
The Granary, North Street, Dorking, Surrey, RH4 1DN
www.templarco.co.uk

Copyright © 2008 by Kevin Waldron

First softback edition

ISBN 978-1-84011-814-8

Edited by Ruth Martin

Printed in china

MR PEEK

AND THE MISUNDERSTANDING

AT THE ZOO

BY KEVIN WALDRON

templar publishing

IT IS ON THE STROKE OF 9AM, MORE OR LESS,
THAT **MR PEEK** THE ZOOKEEPER
GETS READY TO DO HIS ROUNDS.
HE PUTS ON HIS *FAVOURITE JACKET* —
IT MAKES HIM FEEL VERY IMPORTANT.

HE NOTICES THAT IT IS **VERY** TIGHT
AND ONE OF THE BUTTONS **POPS OFF!**
THIS IS NOT A GOOD START TO HIS DAY
BUT HE SETS OFF NONETHELESS.

"It's only a
button!"

"Oh woe is me!
You're getting very fat,"

MR PEEK SAYS TO **HIMSELF**,
NOTICING THE BULGE IN HIS JACKET.

THE **HIPPO** OVERHEARS
AND THINKS THE REMARK
IS INTENDED FOR
HER!

"All that terrible food you eat will be the end of you!"

MR PEEK PROCLAIMS AS HE PASSES THE PENGUIN'S POOL. HEARING WHAT HE SAID, THE PENGUINS ALL LOOK AT EACH OTHER **IN HORROR**. THEY HAD **JUST** FINISHED BREAKFAST!

"Why, you're sweating just doing your rounds,"

MR PEEK SAYS TO **HIMSELF** AS HE APPROACHES THE **BEAR'S** CAVE.

"You stink!"

HE **EXCLAIMS**.

"You're getting old too – look how wrinkly you are,"

DECLARES MR PEEK TO HIMSELF
AS HE PASSES THE ELEPHANTS.

"If they think you're too old for this job,
they'll fire you!"

HE SIGHS AS HE PASSES THE **CROCODILE** PIT.

MR PEEK CHECKS ON THE **MONKEYS**,
MUTTERING TO HIMSELF,
"They're all out to get you."

"You can't turn your back for a **moment!**"

"Maybe it won't even come to that,"

HE **SULKS** TO HIMSELF AS HE NEARS THE **TORTOISE'S** GARDEN,

"You could get run down by a rhino tomorrow!"

"Would anybody even care?"

MR PEEK ASKS HIMSELF ALOUD,
SURROUNDED BY GIRAFFES.

"None of the animals even like you!"

"Oh, woe is me!"

MR PEEK CONTINUES, FEELING VERY SORRY FOR HIMSELF.

TURNING A CORNER, HE SEES HIS SON JIMMY
SWEEPING THE PATH IN A VERY LARGE JACKET
THAT REACHES DOWN TO THE GROUND.

JIMMY LOOKS AT HIS DAD AND LAUGHS,

"YOU HAVE **MY** JACKET ON, DAD!"

MR PEEK AND JIMMY SWAP THEIR JACKETS.
JIMMY'S JACKET IS **MISSING A BUTTON**,
BUT HE CAN SEE THE FUNNY SIDE OF IT.
MR PEEK IS VERY RELIEVED.

"See you at home for lunch, son."

HE SAYS **CHEERILY**,
AND SETS OFF AGAIN.

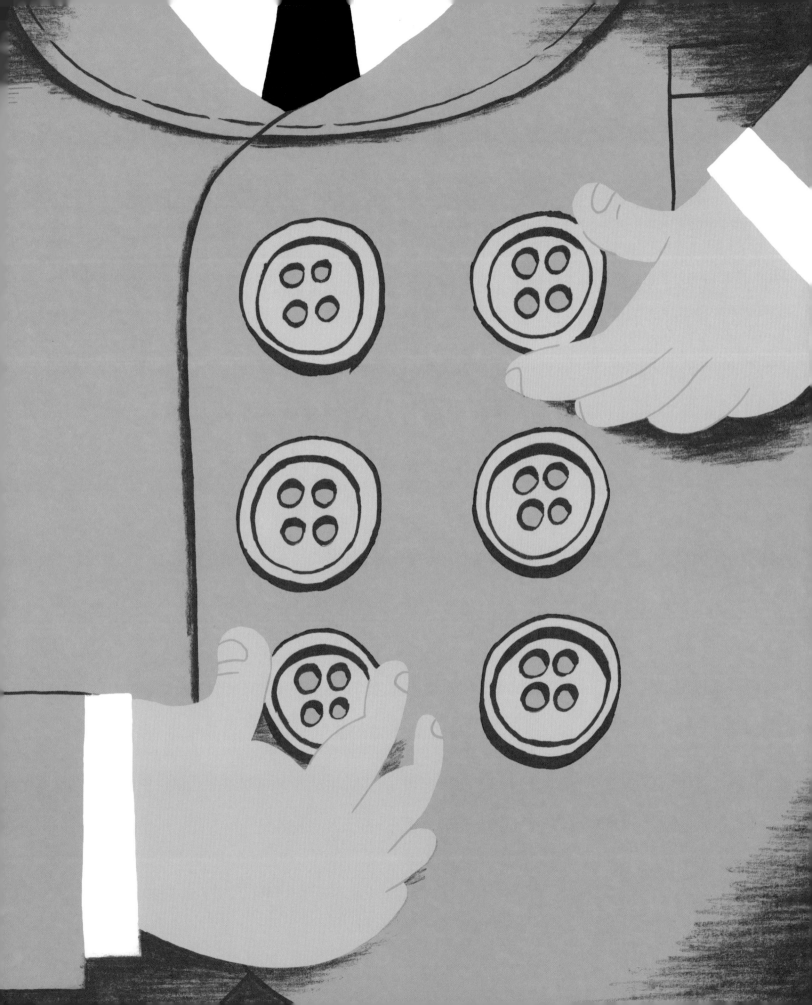

"I guess you're **not** so fat after all!

In fact, you're in pretty good shape

for someone your age,"

MR PEEK SAYS TO HIMSELF

AS HE MAKES HIS WAY BACK HOME.

THE HIPPO WAS MUCH HAPPIER

WITH **THAT**.

"You don't smell bad at all –
no need to worry about that."

A **REASSURED** BEAR
STEPS OUT OF HER CAVE!

"You're not too wrinkly either."

"You look fine just the way you are."

THE ELEPHANTS FLAP THEIR LARGE EARS AND TRUMPET WITH DELIGHT.

"You were foolish to think that they are always watching you!"

WHEN THE CROCODILES **HEAR** THIS
THEY **RELAX** AND **LAUGH** AT THEMSELVES.

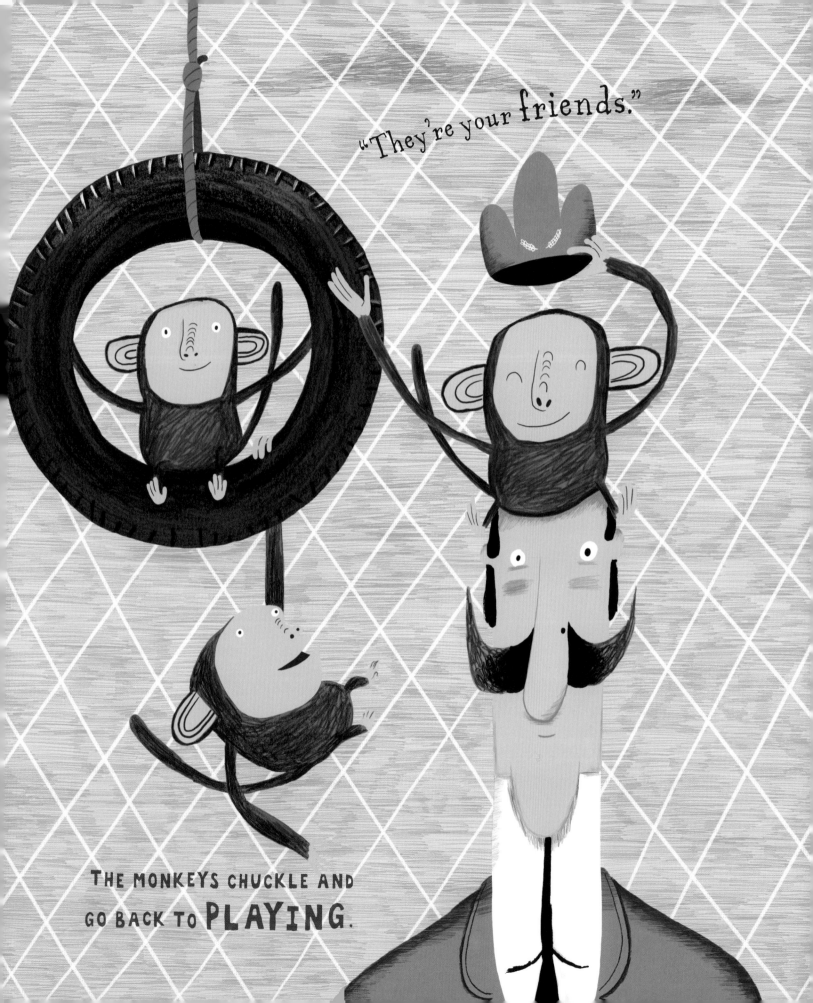

"You're fit and healthy – why worry?"

"PHEW!"

THE GIRAFFES WERE STILL FEELING BLUE,

UNTIL MR PEEK PASSED BY AND SAID...

"All the animals
are like family to you.
There is no reason
to **doubt** that."

"All's well with the world,"

THOUGHT MR PEEK, **PLEASED** TO SEE
THE ANIMALS LOOKING SO CHEERFUL.
HE HAD THOUGHT THEY LOOKED A
LITTLE **GLUM** EARLIER ON...

MR PEEK PROMISED HIMSELF THAT HE
WOULDN'T GET **SO CARRIED AWAY** AGAIN.
HE REACHED INTO HIS POCKET
FOR HIS KEYS...

BUT THEY WERE **NOT** THERE!

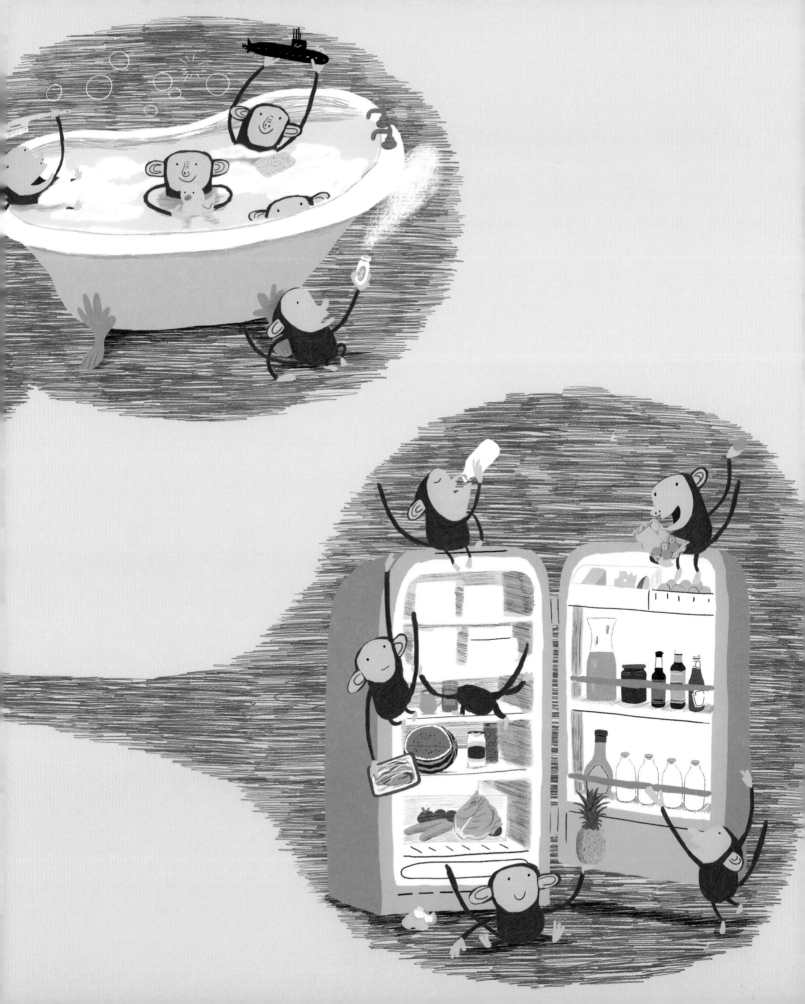

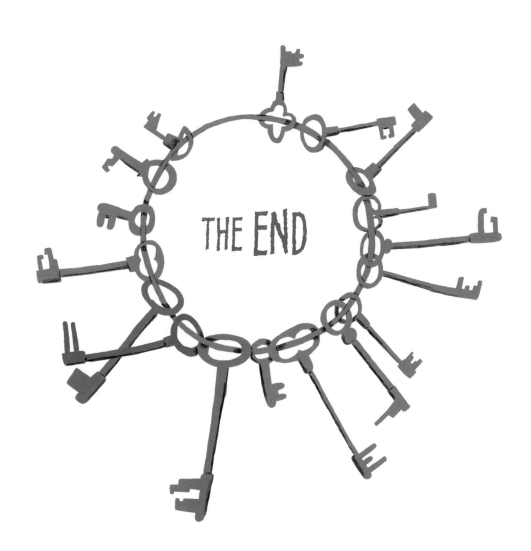

THE END